BE YOU

WRITTEN BY SANDREAN HYMAN-HOWARD
ILLUSTRATED BY LEONDRAE (TY) BROWN

Watersprings
PUBLISHING

BE YOU written by Sandrean Hyman-Howard and Illustrated by Leondrae (Ty) Brown
Published by Watersprings Publishing,
a Division of Watersprings Media House, LLC.
P.O. Box 1284 Olive Branch, MS 38654
www.waterspringspublishing.com
Contact the publisher for bulk orders and permission requests.

Copyright © 2024 Sandrean Hyman-Howard. All rights reserved.

No part of this publication may be reproduced, distributed, or transmitted in any form or by any means, including photocopying, recording, or other electronic or mechanical methods, without the prior written permission of the publisher, except in the case of brief quotations embodied in critical reviews and certain other noncommercial uses permitted by copyright law.

Printed in the United States of America.

ISBN-13: 978-1-964972-03-9

DEDICATED TO:

TY AND SERREN

NIECE AND NEPHEWS

You are fearfully and wonderfully made.

You are unique and special.

BE YOU.

You are talented and creative.

You are smart and intelligent.

You are loved and loveable.

You are honest, kind, and caring.

BE YOU.

You have a voice and a mind of your own.

You are a leader, and you can help others to do well.

You have great potential, and your dreams will take you very far.

You are compassionate and empathetic.

No one else looks, walks, or talks like you.

Do not be influenced to change from positive to negative.

Trust God as He continues to allow you to...

about the author

Sandrean Hyman-Howard

Sandrean is a wife, mother, and a dedicated Christian and a teacher by profession who has spent over ten years in the classroom. She has a passion for imparting knowledge, helping, and encouraging others. She gets excited whenever she gets the privilege to share the goodness of God with others. Prayer is the most important part of her life, and she sincerely believes that prayer changes things for her and everyone else. She believes that positive affirmations and positive self-talk are important daily as this will help our children to think positively about themselves and build powerful self-confidence. Words are very powerful, and having a strong mind helps our children know that they are a very special gift to the world and are *fearfully and wonderfully made in the image of Christ.'* Psalm 139:14.